Before you start to read:
It's a good idea to talk about the front cover and title. Get some ideas about what the book is about, and look at the pictures to generate some interest. Setting the scene like this involves your child and helps her to focus on the story.

How to use the book:
On each page there is a short text, with a bright, eye-catching picture which links in to that part of the story.

On selected pages, you will find a question; some of these can be used to check your child's understanding of the story as you go along; others are designed to focus your child's attention on the shape or sound of letters. Use them as you feel fit; a tired child may just want the story on its own.

In addition, you will note that sometimes characters have been given speech bubbles. These can also be used as a tool to fire your child's imagination; for a change, use the pictures as a springboard for creating a mini drama, acting out the story instead of reading it; the speech bubbles will help you keep on track. You may well discover that you have a talented actor or actress in the family!

3

Sleeping Beauty

Published by

Rewritten by Claire Black

ISBN: 978-1-906068-61-5

ong ago, in a faraway land, a beautiful little girl was born.

She was the daughter of the ruling King and Queen, and was the loveliest Princess ever seen.

The King and Queen were so delighted with their little daughter that they decided to have a party to celebrate.

They had many friends throughout the land and wanted to invite them all.

"We shall invite everyone we know! And we will ask the seven good fairies to be her Godmothers!" decided the Queen.

The King liked the good fairies very much and agreed with the Queen's decision.

The day of the party soon arrived. Everyone dressed in their best outfits; lords and ladies from across the land came to celebrate the birth of the new Princess.

When everyone had arrived, the fairy Godmothers stepped forward and granted a special wish for the little girl.

The first fairy spoke up. "She shall be as beautiful as a rose in bloom," she said.

Everyone clapped and cheered on hearing these words.

Then the second fairy stepped forward with her wish. "She shall be as musical as the strings of a harp," she added.

A moment later the third fairy spoke. "She shall be as rich as gold," she promised.

The fourth, fifth and sixth fairies in turn gave their wishes.

"She shall be as sweet as the fruit from the trees."

"She shall be as wise as the wisest of owls."

"She shall know more happiness than she can imagine."

Just as the sixth fairy had finished speaking, there was a piercing scream from the back of the room. A furious fairy then forced her way through the astonished crowd.

"What about ME?" she shrieked. "You did not invite me to the party and for this I will NOT forgive you! "

Everyone gasped when they saw who was speaking; it was the wicked fairy from the north who had the most evil powers imaginable.

Why was the wicked fairy angry?

She continued screeching at the King and Queen. "I will cast an evil spell over your daughter, one that you will never forget! On her sixteenth birthday, your precious Princess will prick her finger on a spinning wheel, and then she will DIE!"

With these words, she turned and fled from the party, leaving the King and Queen in tears.

Just then, the seventh good fairy stepped forward to speak to the tearful parents.

"Do not despair, for I still have my one wish left; with this, I can change the spell of the evil fairy," she said, soothingly.

"I promise that, if she does prick her finger, she will not die, but will fall into a deep sleep which will last for one hundred years," she continued.

As the years went by, the Princess grew into an adorable, charming girl. The good fairies' wishes had all come true and she was the most beautiful, sweet and happy Princess anyone had ever seen.

But her parents could never forget the words of the evil fairy. As their daughter's sixteenth birthday approached, they began to get more and more worried.

The Princess's birthday was a few months away when the King decided to take some action.

"Destroy all the spinning wheels and needles in the palace," he ordered.

By doing this, he hoped to remove all chance of his daughter ever pricking her finger.

When two letters are next to each other in one word, we call them 'doubles'.
How many double letters can you see on this page?

The Princess' birthday finally arrived. The King and Queen held a wonderful party for their daughter.

Everyone gasped in delight as she appeared on the balcony to greet them, for she had never looked so beautiful.

The young Princess danced all evening. But she soon decided she needed a rest.

"I must step outside for some fresh air," she said to herself.

As she stood in the pale moonlight, she noticed a bright light shining from a tall tower in the distance. She hadn't seen the tower before, so decided to find out more about this strange light.

The Princess made her way to the tower.She climbed right to the top where she came across a huge wooden door. She pushed it open; in front of her was an old woman, sitting at a spinning wheel.

Curious to see what this wheel did, she reached out to touch it - and pricked her finger!

She immediately fell to the floor and into a deep sleep.

The old woman was, of course, the evil fairy. "Ha ha!" she cried in delight, on seeing the Princess asleep. "I told them I would do it!" and she disappeared into the night.

Just then, the good fairy appeared, and cast a spell making everyone in the land fall asleep too.

Years went by. All was quiet; nothing stirred within the palace walls.

Outside, the trees grew tall and the forests grew thick. The gardens around the palace became a tangled wood.

It wasn't many years before the palace almost disappeared from sight. The trees were so dense that no one could possibly find their way through.

The Princess remained asleep in the tower; she became known as Sleeping Beauty.

Why did people find it hard to see the palace?

One day, a handsome Prince came riding through this land. He had heard the story of Sleeping Beauty and wanted to see whether what he had heard was true.

His friends tried to stop him but he was determined to set out on his adventure.

"I will not stop until I have found the palace and seen for myself the beautiful Princess," he said.

He climbed on his horse and set off in the direction of the palace. He did not know how far away it was or how to find it, but he was a brave Prince and he would not give up easily.

The Prince rode for many weeks, through thick forests and overgrown woods. At last he spotted the palace in the distance, almost hidden from sight.

"How long has this wood been growing around the palace?" he wondered.

But in his heart he knew the answer. Sleeping Beauty had been asleep for one hundred years.

As the Prince started cutting his way through the woods, something magical happened: a sharp wind began to blow, slicing the forest away to reveal a path in front of him.

The wind had been sent by the seventh good fairy; she was helping the Prince find his way to the palace!

What did the seventh fairy do to help the Prince?

In no time at all, the Prince was able to take the path right to the palace doors. On seeing a light at the top of the nearby tower, he dashed up the stairs.

He threw open the wooden door; there, in front of him, was the beautiful Sleeping Beauty. With one quick movement, he bent down to kiss the sleeping girl.

With this kiss, the spell was broken; Sleeping Beauty opened her eyes and smiled at the handsome Prince.

Just then, everyone else in the palace awoke. The King and Queen rushed to the tower and found their daughter in the arms of the noble Prince.

Sleeping Beauty had been saved. The Prince and she married the very next day and lived happily ever after.